Selena
the Sleepover Fairy

Special thanks
to Rachel Elliot

ORCHARD BOOKS

First published in Great Britain in 2011 by Orchard Books
This edition published in 2018 by The Watts Publishing Group

15

Copyright © 2018 Rainbow Magic Limited.
Copyright © 2018 HIT Entertainment Limited.
Illustrations copyright © Orchard Books 2011 HIT entertainment

A CIP catalogue record for this book is available from the British Library.

ISBN 978 1 40831 285 8

Printed and bound by Clays Ltd, Elcograf S.p.A

MIX
Paper from
responsible sources
FSC® C104740

The paper and board used in this book are made from wood from responsible sources

Orchard Books
An imprint of Hachette Children's Group
Part of The Watts Publishing Group Limited
Carmelite House, 50 Victoria Embankment, London EC4Y 0DZ

An Hachette UK Company
www.hachette.co.uk
www.hachettechildrens.co.uk

Selena
the Sleepover
Fairy

by Daisy Meadows

ORCHARD

The Fairyland Palace

Service Station

← Coach

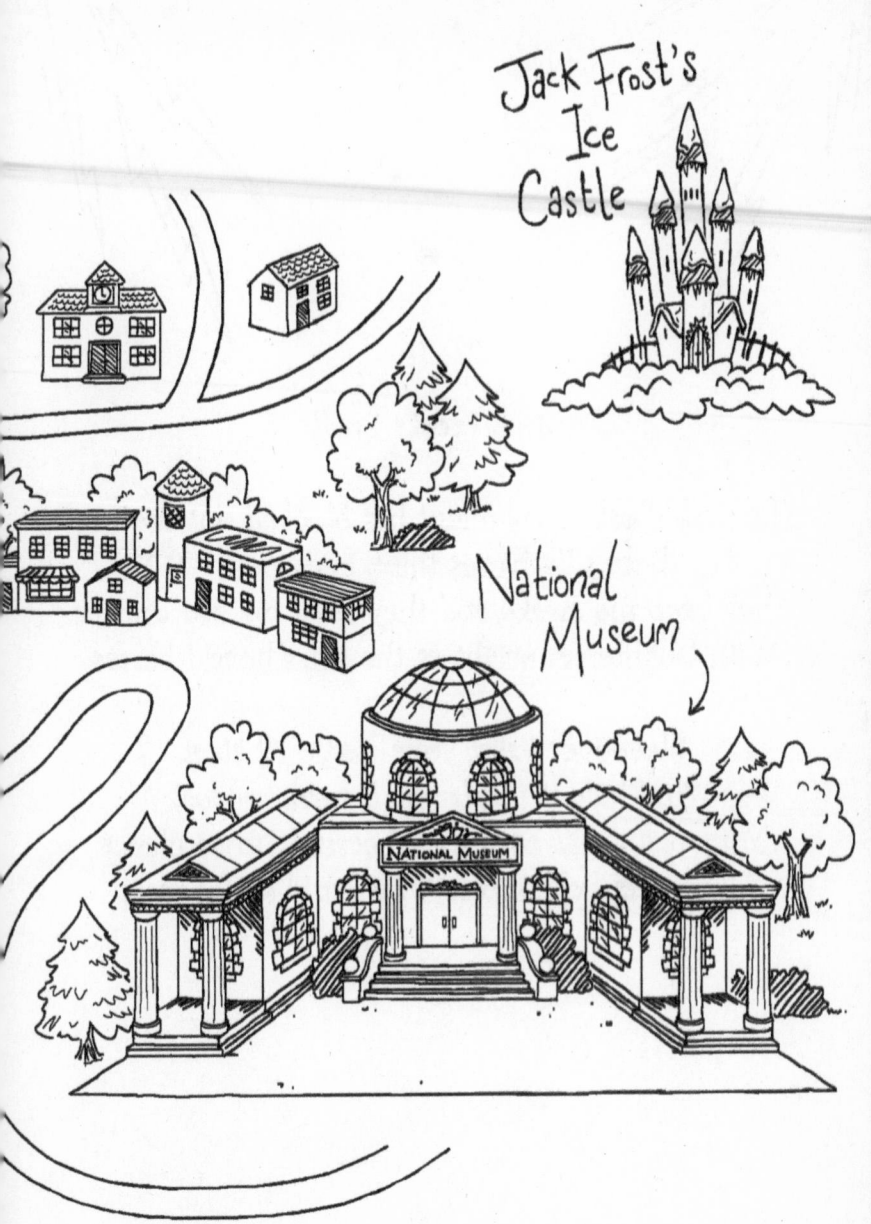

Jack Frost's Spell

The dark cloak of midnight has blocked out the sun,
But those silly fairies think bedtime is FUN!
They keep me awake and they spoil my bad dreams
With laughter as bright as the sun's horrid beams.

Sleepover Fairy, your magic I'll steal,
And hide it in places I'll never reveal.
Your plans will be ruined because I'm so clever.
And sleepover fun will be banished forever!

The Magical Sleeping Bag

Contents

School Trip

"I feel as if it's my birthday and Christmas at the same time!" said Rachel Walker, bouncing up and down on her coach seat. "I can't believe we're actually going to a sleepover in the National Museum!"

"It makes it twice as exciting that you're here," her best friend Kirsty Tate agreed, settling down beside her. "It was so kind of the headmaster to let you come along."

Kirsty's school had won a place in a giant eco-charity sleepover, which was being held in the National Museum. Thirty children from the school were going to the city to take part. Rachel was staying with Kirsty, and so she had been allowed to join in, too.

The coach driver took his place and the engine rumbled into life. As the coach drew out of the school car park, the girls waved goodbye to Kirsty's mum, who had come to see them off.

"I hope it's not spooky there at night," said a girl called Hannah, who was sitting in the seat behind Rachel. "I'm a bit scared of the dark."

"Don't worry," said Kirsty with a comforting smile. "I've been there before and it's really cool. There are loads of amazing things to do."

"I want to see the dinosaur gallery!" said Rachel, opening a bag of sweets and offering them round.

"Ooh yes, and the diamonds exhibition with all the sparkling gems and jewels," Kirsty added, taking a pink bonbon and popping it into her mouth.

"The marine fossils!" said Arthur.

"The wildlife garden!" said Ali.

"The world lab!" said Dan.

Suddenly there was a loud bang from underneath their feet.

"What was that?" Hannah squealed. "Has a wheel come off?"

"I don't think so," said Rachel, frowning. "It sounded as if it was inside the coach."

Their teacher, Mr Ferguson, stood up at the front of the coach.

"Don't worry, everyone," he said. "It's just our bags slipping and sliding around in the luggage hold. I hope you don't have any eggs in your rucksacks!"

There was a little ripple of laughter and Hannah looked less nervous.

"Come on," said Kirsty, trying to take Hannah's mind off her fears. "Let's play a game."

Soon Rachel, Kirsty and their friends were having a fun and noisy game of snap. They hardly heard the occasional bangs and thumps from the luggage hold and they didn't notice when the coach joined the motorway. When it started to slow down, they looked around in surprise.

"Are we there already?" asked Kirsty.

"Not yet," said Mr Ferguson with a smile. "We're going to have a comfort break. We'll be setting off in twenty minutes, so keep an eye on your watches. Everyone must be back here by quarter past seven."

Everyone filed off the coach. Kirsty and Rachel were the last to step off. As they hurried after the others, Kirsty noticed that her shoelace was undone. She bent down to tie it up, and Rachel waited for her.

"It's nicer here than most service stations," she said. "I like all the greenery."

The service station was hidden from the motorway by a line of leafy trees. As Rachel looked at them, something sparkled among the leaves. Rachel gasped.

"Kirsty, look up there!"

Kirsty stood up and clutched Rachel's hand in excitement.

"That looks like fairy dust!" she exclaimed. "Oh Rachel, do you think we're about to have another adventure?"

"Let's find out!" Rachel said.

The girls hurried towards the trees. They were friends with the fairies who lived in Fairyland, and often helped out when mischievous Jack Frost caused trouble. Could it be that the fairies needed their help again?

Fairy Sparkles

As soon as the girls were among the trees, the sparkles became brighter and whooshed towards them like a miniature shooting star. The blur of lights whirled around Rachel and Kirsty in glimmering hoops of purple and pink. Then the blur slowed down, and the girls saw a fairy hovering in front of them, her long, plaited black hair gleaming in the evening sun.

She was wearing a pretty white playsuit trimmed in pink, and there were pink fluffy slippers on her feet. Under her arm was a little teddy bear.

"Hello," she said in a velvety, soft voice. "I'm Selena the Sleepover Fairy."

"It's lovely to meet you," said Rachel with a smile. "We're on our way to a giant sleepover!"

"Yes, I know," said Selena, looking worried. "That's why I'm here. Your sleepover could be at risk. Jack Frost has done something horrible!"

"What do you mean?" Kirsty gasped.

"What's happened?" asked Rachel.

Selena fluttered over to a low branch and perched on a nodding leaf.

"The Twilight Fairies and I organised a midsummer fairy sleepover last night," she explained. "It was so much fun! All the fairies were there, and there were games, songs, stories and snacks."

"It sounds lovely," said Kirsty.

"Jack Frost didn't think so," said Selena.

"He got cross because we were having so much fun. While we were playing games in the starlight, he sneaked into the meadow where we were planning to sleep."

Rachel's hand flew to her mouth.

"What did he do?" she asked.

Selena bit her lip.

"He stole my most precious possessions!" she said. "He knows that my three magical objects help sleepovers to go smoothly. Without them, last night was ruined. And now your giant sleepover at the museum might be, too!"

"What are your magical objects?" Rachel asked.

Selena smiled as she thought about them.

"The Magical Sleeping Bag ensures that everyone gets a good night's sleep," she said. "The Enchanted Games Bag makes all games fun and fair, and the Sleepover Snack Box guarantees everyone will enjoy lots of delicious food."

"Oh my goodness," said Kirsty. "Without games and food, sleepovers will be spoiled!"

"Couldn't you ask Jack Frost to give them back?" Rachel suggested.

"I did," said Selena sadly. "I went to the Ice Castle to beg him to return my precious things. I even told him about your charity sleepover. But he just said that if human sleepovers were spoiled as well, that would make him even happier!"

Kirsty and Rachel had been to Jack Frost's Ice Castle during other fairy adventures. It was a very scary place – the little fairy had been very brave to visit it all by herself. Kirsty squeezed Rachel's hand and gave Selena a reassuring smile.

"Please try not to worry," she said.
"We'll help you to find your magical
objects. We'll do everything we can to get
them back."

"Thank you!" said Selena. "The
Twilight Fairies told me how kind you
are. They suggested I should come and
find you."

"The hardest part is knowing where to
start looking," said Kirsty thoughtfully.
"Perhaps we should visit the castle
ourselves and search for
clues."

"I don't think
we need to
do that,"
said Rachel,
sounding excited.
"Look over there!"

Selena and Kirsty turned to look where Rachel was pointing, and their mouths fell open. Six goblins were climbing out of the luggage hold of their coach, carrying armfuls of rucksacks and sleeping bags!

"Those naughty goblins!" exclaimed Kirsty. "Why do they want our things?"

As the girls watched, the green
mischief-makers scampered into the
service station, laden down with their
luggage for the sleepover.

"They'll be seen!" exclaimed Rachel.
"Come on, we have to follow them!"

A Goblin Sleepover

Kirsty, Rachel and Selena hurried into the service station after the goblins. It was crowded with people, and Selena tucked herself out of sight under Kirsty's hair. On their left was a self-service cafe, where their schoolfriends were buying drinks and snacks. On their right was a shop, and a sign pointed to the toilets straight ahead.

"Where did they go?" whispered Selena in Kirsty's ear.

The service station was so busy that it was hard to see through the crowds. Kirsty and Rachel looked all around, and then Rachel gave a cry. Among the crowds, she had spotted a green sleeping bag bobbing in the air. A goblin was carrying it on his head!

"That way – look!"

The girls pushed their way through the jostling crowds, dodging elbows, bags and legs. They kept catching glimpses of the goblins ahead of them, and squabbling goblin voices floated back to them.

"Get off my sleeping bag!"

"That pink rucksack's mine."

"Give it back!"

The goblins were pushing each other crossly. One of them staggered sideways into a magazine stand and knocked it over. The shop manager gave an angry shout. Kirsty was so busy trying to see what was happening, she forgot to look where she was going. Suddenly she ran into a very large man!

"Ooof!" he said in surprise, as Kirsty stumbled backwards into Rachel.

"Ooof!" said Rachel.

"Ooh, sorry!" Kirsty exclaimed. "Are you OK?"

"No harm done," said the man with a jolly smile.

But when the girls looked around again, the goblins had completely disappeared!

"Oh no," groaned Rachel. "How are we going to find them now?"

"I've got an idea," said Selena.

She gave her wand a tiny flick, and it began to glow.

"This spell will make the wand glow brighter the closer we are to the goblins," she whispered in Kirsty's ear. "Just keep walking and I'll tell you which way to go."

Guided by the glowing wand, they hurried towards the back of the service station until they reached an escalator. They could see only shadows beyond the escalator. Even the lights weren't working.

"There's nothing here," said Rachel, looking around. "No shops, no cafes – it's just a bit dark and spooky."

Just then, the girls heard a giggle. Raising a finger to her lips, Kirsty tiptoed around the back of the escalator. The tip of Selena's wand was glowing very brightly indeed. Rachel followed, and together they put their heads around the corner.

The goblins were all there, sitting on the ground! They had rolled out their stolen sleeping bags and were searching through the rucksacks for nightclothes.

"Jack Frost will never guess where we are," giggled one of the goblins.

He pulled on a pink feathery eye mask and settled back with a contented sigh.

"I'm not ready to go to sleep yet," said another goblin, who was wearing checked pyjamas. "When do the games start?"

"Where is everyone?" asked a third goblin, looking around expectantly. "Maybe they're playing hide and seek."

He paced around, peering into the

shadows. The girls drew back a little, feeling puzzled. Why would the goblins think there were going to be games in a service station?

"It was lucky we heard that fairy telling Jack Frost about the humans' giant sleepover," said another goblin, pulling on fluffy orange bedsocks. "I've always wanted to go to one."

"Oh!" exclaimed Rachel with a flash of understanding. "They must have decided to gatecrash our sleepover, and they think this is it!"

"In the middle of a service station?" said Kirsty. "Oh dear, those silly goblins!"

The goblins were already quarrelling.

"Shut up and go to sleep!" snapped the eye-mask goblin.

"But I'm not sleepy," squeaked the

goblin in the checked pyjamas.

"This is no fun," said a skinny goblin who was wearing an old-fashioned nightcap. "Sleepovers are boring!"

"You're boring!" snapped the goblin with the bedsocks.

A teddy bear flew through the air and hit the skinny goblin on the nose.

"YOWCH!" he squawked. "You'll be sorry you did that!"

Selena darted out from under Kirsty's hair with a cry of excitement.

"Look at his sleeping bag!" she said, pointing at the skinny goblin.

Rachel and Kirsty peered through the gloom. The sleeping bag didn't suit the goblin at all. It was pink and decorated with hearts and sweets, and it was glowing with a soft, warm light.

"Rachel, Kirsty, that's my Magical Sleeping Bag!" Selena told them, her eyes shining. "We've found it!"

A Smelly Spell

Rachel and Kirsty gasped as they stared at the Magical Sleeping Bag. The skinny goblin was snuggling down into it.

"We can't get it back while he's in it," Rachel whispered.

Kirsty checked her watch.

"We only have eight minutes left before we're due back at the coach!" she said. "How are we going to get the Magical Sleeping Bag back in time?"

"Perhaps if we asked them nicely they might give it back," said Selena.

Rachel shook her head.

"They'll never agree to that," she said. "They never do anything unless there's something in it for them."

"I've got an idea," said Kirsty in a low voice. "Selena, could you do a spell to make the sleeping bag really uncomfortable for the goblin?"

"Oh, that's a wonderful idea!" said Rachel. "If he's not comfy in the sleeping bag, he'll get out of it, and we'll be able to grab it."

"I know just the spell!" said Selena with a smile.

Peeping around the corner, she waved her wand.

"Rosy posy, soft and cosy," she said

under her breath.

A ribbon of shimmering fairy dust
coiled towards the Magical Sleeping Bag.
The girls watched and held their breath.

Suddenly the skinny goblin started to
squirm and wriggle.

"My sleeping bag smells funny,"
he complained. "Yuck! It stinks of
strawberries!"

"Ugh, what a pong!" said the goblin
next to him, holding his nose. "I can smell
roses!"

Rachel and Kirsty had to cover their mouths to stop their giggles being heard.

"There are flower petals in here!" cried the skinny goblin. "This stupid fairy sleeping bag is full of horrible fairy sweetness. Get me out of here!"

He crawled out of the sleeping bag, his nose wrinkled in disgust.

"Now's our chance!" said Rachel.

She and Kirsty ran towards the empty sleeping bag with Selena fluttering by their side.

"It's those interfering girls again!" squeaked the goblin with the orange bedsocks. "Don't let them take the bag!"

All the goblins leapt towards the Magical Sleeping Bag except for the one wearing the eye mask, who blundered in the opposite direction. The skinny goblin grabbed his arm and dragged him along too. Before the girls could reach it, all six goblins were scrambling into the Magical Sleeping Bag.

"Yah! You're not taking our sleeping bag!" they called out.

Selena fluttered to the ground in front of them.

"It's not your sleeping bag," she said firmly. "You shouldn't try to keep what doesn't belong to you."

"Can't hear you!" jeered the skinny goblin, sticking his fingers in his ears.

"That sleeping bag belongs to Selena!" exclaimed Rachel, her hands on her hips. "Give it back!"

The goblins zipped up the sleeping bag until all that could be seen of them was six green heads poking out at the top. They were all sticking out their tongues at the girls and pulling faces.

"All right," said Selena with a cheeky smile. "If you want to stay in the Magical Sleeping Bag, I'll help you."

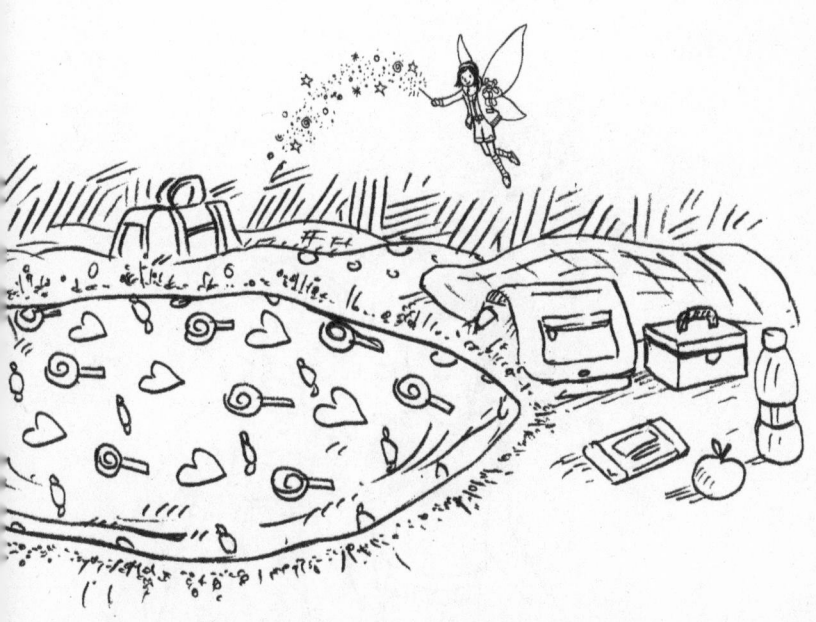

She made a rainbow-shaped sweeping motion over the bag, and then winked at Rachel and Kirsty.

"This sleeping bag is horribly soft and feathery!" complained the eye-mask goblin. "I want to get out!"

"I can't undo the zip!" cried the goblin in checked pyjamas.

"That tricksy fairy's magicked it shut!" said another goblin in a panic. "We're stuck!"

The goblins writhed and wriggled and squawked, but they couldn't get out of the sleeping bag. Rachel and Kirsty giggled and Selena hovered above the goblins.

"Now," she said. "Are you goblins ready to make a deal?"

All Aboard!

"We'll never give you the bag!" shouted one goblin.

"Jack Frost would shout at us for a month and shut us in the dungeons!" said another.

"But I'm guessing you've taken the Magical Sleeping Bag without his permission," Rachel said thoughtfully. "I expect he's already cross with you."

"How did she know that?" whispered the eye-masked goblin loudly.

"You don't like this fairy sleeping bag, do you?" asked Selena.

Six green heads waggled from side to side.

"It's smelly!" said one.

"It's too soft!" said another.

"I could make you each a wonderful goblin sleeping bag," said Selena. "All you have to do is give back the Magical Sleeping Bag and all the ordinary sleeping bags and rucksacks that don't belong to you."

The goblins went quiet. Their heads moved closer together as they whispered and argued.

Kirsty bit her lip anxiously. The seconds were ticking by, and it was almost time for them to be back at the coach. They couldn't leave the goblins here in the service station!

Then she noticed that a goblin in a pair of polka-dot pyjamas was looking very red in the face. Beads of sweat were forming on his forehead.

"I'm too hot!" he moaned. "It's too squashed in here. You can have the sleeping bag. Just let me out!"

"Yes, let us out!" shouted the other goblins. "We agree! We agree!"

With a wave of her wand, Selena freed the zip and the hot, perfumed goblins tumbled out of the bag. They kicked it over to the girls.

"Now you keep your side of the bargain!" demanded the skinny goblin.

"Of course," said Selena with a big smile.

There were six loud popping noises, and each goblin found a stinky green sleeping bag under his arm. They all sniffed eagerly.

"Mmm, cabbages!" said the eye-mask goblin.

"Mouldy fruit!" squeaked another.

"Mine's all scrunchy," said the goblin with the orange bedsocks. "I think it's full of thistles. Yippee!"

And with that, the goblins rushed off in the direction of the car park.

The girls turned to Selena.

"Can you magic them back to the Ice Castle?" asked Kirsty. "I don't like the idea of taking them to the giant sleepover!"

"I'm sorry," said Selena. "My magic isn't strong enough for that. But as soon as I've returned the Magical Sleeping Bag to its rightful home, I'll come back to help you at the sleepover. After all, we still have to find my other two magical objects!"

Selena tapped her wand gently on the Magical Sleeping Bag. With a flurry of glistening sparkles it returned to fairy-size. Another wave of her wand sent all the ordinary sleeping bags and rucksacks back to the coach.

"I've made sure that all the goblins will sleep for the rest of the journey, so they'll stay out of trouble," she said. "Thank you so much for helping me, both of you. I'll be back as soon as I can to help you look for the snack box and the games bag so all sleepovers can be fun and happy once again."

"We'll do whatever we can to help,"
Rachel promised with a big smile.

As Selena disappeared in a swirl of
shimmering fairy dust, Kirsty looked at
her watch.

"Oh no, we've only got thirty seconds
until we're due back at the coach!" she
said. "Rachel – run!"

The girls pelted back through the
service station, dodging the crowds of
people. They ran to the coach, climbed
on board and dropped into their seats,
panting and giggling.

"Cutting it fine, girls," said Mr Ferguson, tapping his watch. "All right, we're all present and correct. Next stop, the National Museum!"

The Enchanted Games Bag

Contents

A Vanishing Act

The coach rolled along a wide street in the centre of the city. Kirsty and Rachel pressed their noses up to the window. It was almost dark, but each tree along the pavement was lit up with sparkling fairy lights.

"I wonder if Selena will be waiting for us inside the museum," said Kirsty quietly.

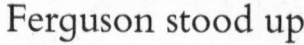

"We still have to find the Enchanted Games Bag and the Sleepover Snack Box so all sleepovers will be fun again!"

The coach pulled up in front of the National Museum. It was very grand indeed! Tall pillars stood on either side of the large entrance, and the words 'National Museum' were carved into the stone above the door. Mr Ferguson stood up.

"We're here!" he announced. "Now remember, there are going to be a lot of different groups at the museum this evening, so stay close to me."

Kirsty and Rachel eagerly filed off the coach. The square in front of the museum was crowded with children, and there were more coaches pulling up all the time. Chatter and laughter filled the air. Kirsty and Rachel held each other's hand tightly and gazed around.

There were some children in school uniform and others in ordinary clothes. The girls saw lots of Cubs, Scouts, Guides and Brownies. Ten children were wearing green T-shirts with 'Northbrooks Junior Choir' printed on them in white letters.

Teachers and group leaders were calling out instructions, and rucksacks and sleeping bags were being hoisted onto shoulders. It was very busy and exciting, and for a moment the girls forgot about everything except watching the crowds of children.

"Right, everybody," said Mr Ferguson in a loud voice, making them jump. "Take your things from the luggage hold and line up in pairs."

"Oh Kirsty!" Rachel exclaimed. "We have to get to the luggage hold and check that the goblins aren't up to mischief!"

"But we're right at the back!" said Kirsty.

The girls tried to squeeze their way to the front, but Mr Ferguson noticed and stopped them.

"No pushing, girls," he said. "Your rucksacks aren't going to walk off by themselves."

"No," said Kirsty under her breath, "but they might walk off with goblin legs underneath them!"

"Selena cast a spell to make them sleep," Rachel reminded her. "I just hope that they will be out of sight at the back of the luggage hold, and nobody will see them."

It seemed to take forever until the children in front of them had collected their bags. At last it was their turn.

Making sure that Mr Ferguson didn't spot them, they picked up their things and peered into the shadows at the back of the luggage hold. The lights from the trees on the pavement lit up the space, and the girls could see that, apart from a few bags, the space was empty!

"There's nothing there!" said Rachel.

"No goblins and no goblin sleeping bags," Kirsty agreed. "But they were supposed to be asleep!"

Rachel remembered something.

"Selena said that her spell would make the goblins sleep 'for the rest of the journey'," she said. "They must have woken up as soon as we arrived at the museum, and climbed out before we got off the coach."

"Maybe they've gone back to the Ice Castle," said Kirsty hopefully.

The girls looked around at the crowds of children heading into the museum. If the goblins were among them, they would be really difficult to spot. Rachel shook her head.

"I don't think they've gone home," she said. "Keep looking out for them, Kirsty. I have a feeling that there's more goblin trouble ahead!"

The Purple Group

Kirsty and Rachel joined the back of the line, and Mr Ferguson led them all into the museum. They found themselves standing in the grand entrance hall. For the moment, all thoughts of goblins left their minds.

The glass dome ceiling seemed to be miles above their heads, and through it they could see the moon and stars shining. The floor was paved with black and white tiles. A flight of wide stone steps curved up to the galleries, and long corridors led off to the sides. In the centre of the hall stood a life-size dinosaur model, its jaws gaping.

"ROOAARRR!"

Everyone squealed and giggled as the recording echoed around the hall. Then a smiling, dark-haired lady walked towards them, holding a clipboard.

"Good evening, children," she said. "My name is Charlotte. I just need to sign you in, and then we can get the fun started."

Mr Ferguson shook hands with Charlotte.

"Thirty children from Wetherbury School," he said.

Charlotte ticked off their names on her clipboard.

"Welcome to the National Museum," she said with a beaming smile. "We're so excited to have you all here. You are going to be in the Purple Group. You can leave your rucksacks and sleeping bags in the left luggage room. It's over there in the corner."

She handed Mr Ferguson a bag of purple caps.

"Everyone must wear one of these to show which group they are in," she said. "The first game will be a gallery treasure hunt, and each group will be in a different gallery. The Purple Group is going to be in the Roman Gallery."

"What sort of treasure are we going to be looking for?" asked Rachel.

"Each group must follow clues to find a letter of the alphabet," Charlotte explained. "When all the letters are put together, they will make the name of a place in the museum. That's where the midnight feast and storytelling will be held!"

It sounded wonderful! There were lots of excited mutters and whispers among the children. But Kirsty felt worried.

"The Enchanted Games Bag is still missing," she whispered to Rachel. "Without it, the treasure hunt game might go wrong, and that would spoil the midnight feast and the storytelling!"

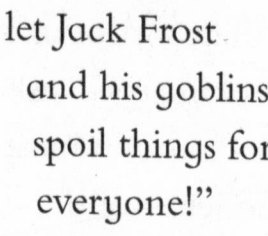

"Don't worry," said Rachel. "We won't let Jack Frost and his goblins spoil things for everyone!"

The girls put their belongings in the left luggage room and Charlotte led the way to the Roman Gallery.

When they reached the gallery, Charlotte handed an envelope to each pair of children.

"Somewhere in here, a letter of the alphabet has been hidden," she said. "It's your mission to find it and bring it to the grand entrance hall. The clues in these envelopes will help you. Good luck, and have fun!"

The children rushed into the Roman Gallery, tearing open the envelopes. Kirsty and Rachel looked around quickly. There was not a goblin in sight.

"They're not here," said Rachel. "Quick, Kirsty – open our clue!"

Kirsty opened the envelope and took out a piece of green card.

"That's funny," said Rachel. "I'd have expected the card to be purple for the Purple Group."

The clue was printed on it:

> HARDER THAN GLASS AND
> RICHER THAN CROWNS
> YOU'LL FIND ME ON FINGERS
> AND FABULOUS GOWNS

"What does it mean?" Kirsty wondered. "Something that's harder than glass... diamonds, perhaps?"

"Yes!" Rachel cried. "They are found on fingers too – in rings!"

"There's a diamond exhibition in the museum," said Kirsty. "Perhaps we're meant to look in there?"

"But Charlotte said that our clues would be about something in here," Rachel replied. "Kirsty, I think something's wrong!"

Treasure Hunt Trouble

Suddenly, a boy in a green cap came running through the door.

"Hey, I think I've got one of your clues by mistake," he announced, holding up a purple card.

"Mr Ferguson, my clue doesn't make sense," said Hannah at the same time. "It's all about sea life."

Everyone started talking at once and holding up their clues. Rachel saw red, green, blue and yellow cards being waved in the air.

"I'm sure that our clues are supposed to be printed on purple card," she said. "I think all the clues have been muddled up."

Kirsty and Rachel looked out through the door. They could see children in different coloured hats running between the galleries. Charlotte was standing in the middle of them all, frantically checking her clipboard.

"This is all because the Enchanted Games Bag is missing," said Rachel in a low voice. "Oh Kirsty, the treasure hunt is going to be ruined. If only there were something we could do."

"Maybe there is," said Kirsty, her eyes shining.

She pointed at the display behind them. One of the ancient Roman vases was glowing! Suddenly, Selena zoomed out of it and waved at the girls through the glass display cabinet. Then, with a tiny flash of fairy dust, she magicked herself out of the cabinet and tucked herself under Rachel's collar.

The girls crouched down behind the display and Selena fluttered out and perched on Kirsty's knee.

"I've got good news!" she said, her cheeks pink with excitement. "I've seen the Enchanted Games Bag! A boy wearing a red cap has it in his travel bag."

"How did he get it?" gasped Kirsty.

"One of the goblins must have dropped it," said Rachel thoughtfully. "I expect the boy saw it and picked it up."

"Let's go and find him now," pleaded Selena.

Rachel and Kirsty nodded, but before they could move they saw a very short child rushing past the door of the Roman Gallery. He was wearing a green cap pulled low over his face, but that didn't fool the girls for one moment.

"That was a goblin!" cried Kirsty.

"Oh no, I hope they haven't got the Enchanted Games Bag back!" said Selena.

"Quick, let's follow him," said Rachel.

"It'll be easier if you're small like me," Selena declared.

The girls ducked into an alcove where they couldn't be seen. Selena waved her wand, and for a moment a shimmering star of fairy dust hung in the air in front of the girls. Then it dissolved into hundreds of

miniature stars that enveloped Rachel and Kirsty in a magical glow. They closed their eyes and felt themselves shrinking to fairy-size, their toes and fingertips tingling pleasantly. When they opened their eyes, they were hovering in the air beside Selena, fluttering their delicate wings.

"Come on," said Rachel. "We have to catch up with that goblin!"

They zoomed out of the Roman Gallery and glimpsed the goblin running down the stone staircase. All the groups and teachers were upstairs and the museum was closed, so the large entrance hall should have been empty. But when the girls reached the bottom of the staircase, they saw that the polished mahogany reception desk was fully staffed – by six goblins!

One was tearing entrance tickets off a long strip, while another was wearing headphones and listening to a guided tour. A third was pressing all the buttons on the till and making them beep. The skinniest goblin was sitting on a revolving seat while another goblin spun him

around at top speed, giggling.

Selena and the girls hid behind a dinosaur model as the goblin in the green cap rushed up to the desk.

"I can't find the pesky human child who picked up the fairy bag," he wailed. "They all look the same to me."

"We'll all have to go and look," said the skinny goblin. "Come on!"

Rachel looked at Kirsty and Selena in alarm.

"We have to find that boy before the goblins do!" she said in an urgent whisper.

They flitted back up to the galleries, and zoomed off in three different directions. This was a race against time!

Finders Keepers

Rachel darted down a long corridor, peering closely at any boy she saw wearing a red cap. But none of them was carrying anything that looked like a magical object. Then she noticed a boy sitting alone on a small bench in the Dinosaur Gallery.

He was wearing a Scout uniform and a red cap, and unlike most of the children he still had his travel bag with him. He unzipped it and pulled out a bottle of water.

As he was drinking, Rachel saw that there was a very faint glow coming from the bag. This had to be the boy who had picked up Selena's Enchanted Games Bag! She zoomed off to look for Kirsty and Selena.

They were both hovering at the top of the stairs, having searched everywhere else.

"I've found him!" Rachel said in excitement. "Follow me!"

But when they flew into the Dinosaur Gallery, they had a terrible shock. A goblin was creeping up behind the boy,

and his little green hand was just about to grab the travel bag!

At the last moment, the boy stood up and picked up his travel bag. The goblin's hand closed on empty air, and the girls heaved sighs of relief.

"That was close," said Kirsty.

"The goblins don't give up that easily," said Rachel. "Look!"

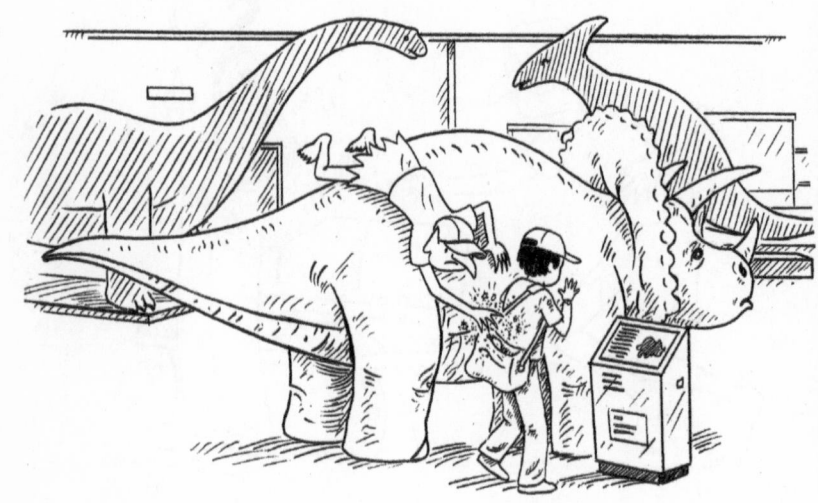

The boy had stopped beside a model of a green-skinned dinosaur. His travel bag was on his back, but he hadn't zipped it up properly. And leaning down from the back of the dinosaur was the goblin in the green hat!

This time the goblin actually got his hand into the bag.

Then the boy seemed to sense that something was wrong. He turned sharply, but the goblin had slid back down behind the dinosaur.

Looking puzzled, the boy strode out of the Dinosaur Gallery. He walked through a small chamber to the Arctic Display. The goblins scurried after him, and the girls fluttered above.

"How are we going to get the Enchanted Games Bag back now?" asked Selena.

The girls could hear the worry in her voice. They put their arms around her.

"Don't worry, Selena," said Kirsty. "If you turn us back into humans, we'll talk to the boy."

"We'll get it back for you," Rachel promised.

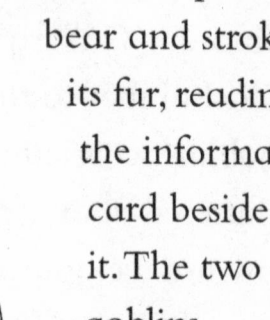

They fluttered to the ground as the boy wandered around the display, reading the descriptions of life in the Arctic Ocean. He paused beside a model of a polar bear and stroked its fur, reading the information card beside it. The two goblins scrambled up the back of the polar bear and teetered on its head. One of them held the other by the ankles and dangled him down towards the bag.

"Oh no, look!" cried Kirsty. "Selena, hurry!"

Selena swept her wand over their heads, and in a flash of fairy dust they were human-sized again. They leapt out in front of the boy, Selena tucking herself under Kirsty's hair.

"Look out!" Rachel shouted.

The boy whipped around and the goblin on top of the polar bear model lost his balance. He let go of the goblin in the green hat, who landed on the ground with a loud squawk of fury.

The first goblin looked scared, and ran out of the room before he could be shouted at.

"Are you trying to steal from me?" the boy demanded crossly. "Leave me alone!"

"Give me that games bag NOW!" demanded the goblin rudely.

The boy looked really angry.

"I don't like people who try to steal from me," he said. "I found that bag, so it's finders keepers!"

Rachel and Kirsty exchanged alarmed looks. What if this boy refused to give the Enchanted Games Bag back to them as well?

A Lesson in Manners

"Excuse me," said Rachel.

The boy turned to look at her.

"Oh, hello," he said. "Thank you for warning me!"

"You're welcome," Rachel replied. "You see, we've been looking for you too. I think you've got something that belongs to a friend of ours."

Kirsty stepped forward with a friendly smile.

"Our friend lost her games bag," she explained. "Without it, lots of children will be really disappointed, because their games won't work properly."

"She really needs it back," Rachel put in. "Please, can you help us?"

The boy stared at them thoughtfully, and then looked at the green-hatted goblin, who was looking very sulky.

"This boy has been trying to take it from me," he said. "It must be very special."

"It is," said Kirsty. "It was stolen from our friend too."

The boy reached into his travel bag and drew out the games bag. He looked at it thoughtfully for a moment. Then he gave a broad smile, and held it out to Rachel.

"It sounds as if your friend needs this more than I do," he said.

"Thank you!" said Rachel and Kirsty together.

With a snort of rage, the goblin ran past the girls and out of the room. The boy raised his eyebrows.

"Maybe that'll teach him a lesson about manners," he said. "I'd better go and find my group. Goodbye!"

"Bye!" called the girls as he hurried out.

Selena flitted out and hovered in front of the girls. With a flick of her wand, the Enchanted Games Bag returned to fairy-size. She smiled at Rachel and Kirsty.

"Thank you for persuading him to give back the bag," she said.

"You're welcome," said Rachel. "Are you going to take the bag back to Fairyland?"

"Yes," Selena replied. "That will fix the treasure hunt problems. But I'll come straight back – we still have to find the Sleepover Snack Box so the midnight feast will be a success."

She smiled and disappeared in a flurry of fairy dust.

"Come on," said Kirsty. "Let's get back to the Roman Gallery."

They walked back to their group. When they arrived, Mr Ferguson was looking very pleased.

"Good news!" he said. "Charlotte has just found some brand-new sets of clues, and our team has already worked out the puzzles. Our letter is C. I'm sorry you missed the chance to solve the clues."

"We don't mind at all," said Rachel, sharing a secret smile with Kirsty.

Now that everything was back to normal, it didn't take long for all the groups to complete their treasure hunts.

Altogether they found five letters. There was a purple C, an orange Y, a blue T, a yellow P and a red R. Everyone gathered in the entrance hall, and Charlotte held up her hand for silence.

"When you put these letters in the right order, they will spell out the place where we're having the midnight feast and storytelling," she said. "Who will be the first to work it out?"

A hand shot into the air. It was the Scout in the red cap – the boy who had found the Enchanted Games Bag.

"It spells 'crypt'," he said.

"Correct," said Charlotte, sounding impressed. "The midnight feast is being held in the old crypt, deep underneath the museum."

Rachel and Kirsty looked at each other, feeling thrilled. A midnight feast in a crypt? How exciting!

The Sleepover Snack Box

Contents

Into the Crypt!

"I can feel butterflies in my tummy, I'm so excited!" whispered Kirsty in Rachel's ear.

Charlotte, the organiser of the museum's giant sleepover, asked everyone to line up in pairs. She handed each of them a little lantern with four glass sides and a curved carrying handle.

"We're about to go down to the crypt, where the midnight feast is being held," she said. "It's dark down there and a little bit spooky, so hold on to your lanterns!"

There were lots of gasps and giggles, and Rachel and Kirsty felt thrilled. They were near the front, and they followed Charlotte down a winding stone staircase to the depths of the museum.

It grew colder and darker as they travelled deeper underground. At last they reached the old, wooden crypt door.

From the hinges, black ironwork stretched across the wood in the shapes of coiling briars and vines. Charlotte pushed the door open, and it gave a loud CREEEAAAK!

"Oooh!" said Hannah, who was standing in front of Rachel.

Charlotte led the way into the dark crypt. A narrow passageway lay in front of them, and the lanterns made shadows flicker across the stone walls.

"This is where we keep all the exhibits that aren't being used," Charlotte said. "The crypt is very, very big, with lots of tunnels leading off from it. We haven't mapped all of them yet, so I don't want anyone going off exploring!"

Rachel and Kirsty saw dark archways on either side of them.

"Where do they lead to?" asked Kirsty.

"Some of the tunnels go right under the city," Charlotte replied.

Her voice echoed around them,
bouncing off the stone walls. Rachel
thought about the long, dark tunnels
stretching underneath the houses and
shops of the city. They sounded very
mysterious and exciting.

The light from their lanterns made
a glowing circle around them as they
walked. The girls saw mysterious boxes
and tall, decorative vases standing on the
floor. There were lots of strange shapes
covered in white dustsheets.

The long snake of children wound through the crypt, passing tall shelves crammed with dusty crates. At last the passageway widened out into a room. In the centre of the room, a man was sitting on an ornate wooden chair with purple cushions. There was a map on the table in front of him.

"Gather round, children!" said Charlotte. "This is Zack the Storyteller, and he will be entertaining you after your midnight feast."

The Storyteller smiled at them. Rachel and Kirsty thought he looked nice. He had twinkling brown eyes that shone in the lamplight, and a long, nut-brown beard.

On the far side of the crypt was a red velvet curtain, which stretched across the whole width of the

room. While
the children
gathered in
a group,
Charlotte
walked
over
to the
curtain
and peered
behind it.

The girls caught a glimpse of a long wooden table before Charlotte let the curtain fall back. When she turned around, she was frowning.

"Charlotte looks worried," Kirsty whispered. "I wonder what's wrong."

Charlotte hurried over to Zack the Storyteller. The girls edged a little closer.

"There's a bit of a problem," they heard Charlotte say. "The picnic food for the feast isn't on the table. Could you start your story early while I go and check what's happened?"

Kirsty and Rachel exchanged alarmed glances.

"Oh no!" said Rachel. "This must be because the Sleepover Snack Box is still missing!"

Selena Appears

"Could everyone sit in a semicircle around the Storyteller, please?" asked Charlotte. "There has been a slight change of plan. The story will start now, before the midnight feast. But don't worry, soon it will be time to eat!"

Her voice sounded reassuring and confident, but Rachel and Kirsty could see worry in her eyes. The other children took their places around the Storyteller, but the girls remained standing as they watched Charlotte leave. They couldn't help worrying about the Sleepover Snack Box. While it was missing, things would keep going wrong with sleepover snacks.

"Sit down, girls," said Mr Ferguson.

Rachel and Kirsty looked around and realised that everyone was waiting for them! They took the only spare places left, which were right at the back of the crowd.

They put their lanterns down, and all the glimmering lights made a large glowing circle around them.

"Welcome to the crypt," said Zack in a rich, warm voice. "This place is full of secrets, and many exciting things have happened here. But most mysterious of all was the puzzle of the museum ghost..."

Rachel started listening to the story, but Kirsty was distracted. She kept thinking that someone was behind her. Eventually she turned her head to look over her shoulder, and glimpsed a spiky-headed shadow!

"Rachel!" she said in an urgent whisper. "Look!"

Rachel looked around, but the strange shadow had completely disappeared.

"What was it?" she asked.

"It was a weird shadow," said Kirsty. "It looked a bit like Jack Frost! I must be imagining things."

"Maybe it was the lights from the lanterns making funny shapes on the wall?" Rachel suggested hopefully.

She looked down at their lanterns and gave a little gasp of surprise. The light in her lantern was fizzing and spluttering. It grew brighter and brighter, then the little glass door shot open and Selena zoomed out from inside!

She fluttered inside Kirsty's jacket so she wouldn't be seen by any of the other children.

"I have news!" she said. "Jack Frost is fed up with the goblins losing things. He

has taken the Sleepover Snack Box himself, and he's determined to hang on to it!"

"Oh Selena, I think he's here!" whispered Kirsty. "I'm sure I just saw his shadow."

Selena nodded, looking worried. "He's searching for the goblins so he can punish them for losing the Magical Sleeping Bag and the Enchanted Games Bag," she said. "I expect he knows they're here, and they're hiding from him."

The girls looked around. Zack was well into his story now, and everyone's attention was on him.

"Nobody will notice if we slip away," said Rachel in a low voice. "Selena, can you turn us into fairies? Then we can fly around the crypt and find out what Jack Frost is up to."

"And try to get the Sleepover Snack Box back," added Kirsty. "He's sure to have it with him!"

"Bring your lanterns," said Selena. "They will help us to search."

The girls crept after Selena into a far corner of the crypt, and then the fairy waved her tiny wand.

There was a faint musical sound like a far-off lullaby, and the girls shrank to the size of fairies, with gossamer wings fluttering on their backs. Their lanterns had shrunk to fairy-size as well.

"We must look like tiny fireflies!" giggled Rachel as they rose up into the air. They fluttered around the edges of the room where the children and Zack were sitting, being careful to stay out of sight.

"I'm glad it's so dark in here," said Kirsty. "Hopefully no one will notice that we're missing."

"Everyone is listening to Zack," said Rachel. "We just have to make sure we're back before the story ends!"

Things Go Bump in the Night

There was a yawning tunnel entrance close by.

"Let's start by looking down there," suggested Kirsty.

Flying as close together as they could, the three friends went slowly down the dark tunnel.

Their tiny lanterns made pinprick shadows against the arched brick roof. Suddenly they saw some bulky shapes on the ground below them.

"What are they?" asked Selena.

"They're big packing cases," said Rachel. "I remember Mum and Dad using the same sort of boxes when we moved house. The museum must have stored away some old exhibits in them."

They flew lower and saw that the packing cases were stacked high in rows. Suddenly they heard a bang and a loud squawk.

"What was that?" cried Kirsty in alarm.

"It sounded like a goblin," said Selena. "Come on!"

They flew even lower, and as their eyes adjusted to the light, they saw a goblin sitting on the ground and rubbing his sore foot.

"What's the matter with you?" snapped another goblin, coming out of the shadows. "Do you want Jack Frost to hear you?"

"I banged my foot!" wailed the first goblin.

There was a crash and a muffled yell from a pile of boxes against the tunnel wall. A third goblin crawled out from among the boxes, rubbing a large red bump on his head.

"A stupid box just fell on me!" he grumbled. "I don't like it down here! You said there was going to be a midnight feast, but it's cold and dark, and I'm hungry."

"You'll feel even worse if Jack Frost catches us!" hissed the first goblin. "Shut up!"

"You can't tell us what to do!" squawked the goblin who had bumped his head.

He flung himself on the first goblin and knocked him down.

The other goblin jumped on top of them both, yelling. Selena looked at the girls. "If Jack Frost were down here, he'd have come running by now," she said. "Come on, let's look somewhere else."

They flew back along the tunnel and out into the main room. As they were fluttering towards the next tunnel, Rachel gave a little cry and quickly put her hand over her mouth.

"I can see Jack Frost!" she whispered to Selena and Kirsty.

Sure enough, Jack Frost was skulking around in the shadows behind the crowd of children. He was edging closer and closer to them... *and the Sleepover Snack Box was tucked under his arm!*

Selena, Rachel and Kirsty zoomed out of sight behind a statue.

"We have to get Jack Frost away from the other children," said Kirsty. "It's a bit spooky down here anyway, and Zack is telling them a ghost story. If they see Jack Frost they'll be really scared."

They fluttered onto the head of another statue and peered around the prongs of its crown. Jack Frost was still stood in the shadows, not moving.

"Why is he just standing there?" asked Selena.

"I think he wants to hear the story," said Rachel suddenly. "He's forgotten all about hunting for the goblins!"

That gave Kirsty an idea.

"Perhaps we should try to remind him about the goblins," she suggested. "That might make him leave the group."

"But how can we do that?" asked Selena.

"Do you think that you could use your magic to make our voices sound like goblins?" asked Kirsty. "Then we could let him hear us talking, and make him follow us."

"Kirsty, that's a brilliant idea!" said Rachel.

"You'll have to make sure he doesn't catch you," said Selena, looking concerned. "It could be dangerous."

"Don't worry," said Rachel with a grin. "I'm sure we can move faster than Jack Frost!"

Midnight Mayhem

Selena waved her wand towards Rachel and Kirsty and whispered a magic spell.

"Squawks and wails and nasty jeers;
Sounds that grate upon the ears.
Hide their sweet and girlish tones
And let Jack Frost hear goblin moans."

Rachel and Kirsty coughed, and then stared at each other.

"Has it worked?" asked Kirsty in a gruff goblin voice.

"Yes!" Rachel said with a squeaky goblin giggle. "Come on, let's lead Jack Frost away from the children!"

Rachel and Kirsty swooped down and perched on a shelf behind Jack Frost. Selena hovered above them to watch what happened.

"He'll never find us!" whispered Kirsty with a goblin-like sneer in her voice.

"Silly old Jack Frost!" said Rachel, giggling.

Jack Frost's head whipped around and the girls pressed themselves back against the wall. His eyes darted this way and that, but of course he couldn't see any goblins.

As soon as he turned back to face Zack, Rachel and Kirsty flew a little further away from him and hid in the folds of a dustsheet.

"Let's hide down here," said Kirsty in her goblin voice.

"I don't like it here – I'm going back to the museum," added Rachel, sounding exactly like a sulky goblin.

Jack Frost turned round again, scowling. He stomped towards them.

"I'm going to teach those goblins a lesson they won't forget!" they heard him mutter.

The girls zoomed into the entrance of a tunnel. They paused beside a dustsheet-covered statue.

"Jack Frost's too much of a scaredy-cat to look for us down here," said Rachel with a goblin snigger.

Jack Frost bared his teeth when he heard this. He took a few steps into the tunnel.

"It's working!" whispered Selena, hovering beside them. "Say something else!"

But just then, Zack reached a very spooky part of his story and he raised his voice. Jack Frost paused and turned to listen.

"The ghost floated towards the unsuspecting children, and..." Zack was saying.

Jack Frost was enthralled. Rachel and Kirsty whispered and giggled like goblins, but he didn't seem to hear them. He was too interested in the story to want to leave!

"Oh no!" cried Rachel. "What are we going to do now?"

They fluttered closer to Jack Frost, who was still rooted to the spot. The Sleepover Snack Box was tucked tightly under his arm.

"We'll just have to try reasoning with him," said Selena.

She lifted her hands helplessly as she said this, and the light from Rachel's lantern cast her shadow onto the wall beside Jack Frost. However, because the wall was curved, it made her shadow giant-sized.

Listening to the scary ghost story, Jack Frost suddenly saw a shadowy monster looming over him, its arms raised high above his head. He gave a choked cry of terror, clutched his spiky head with both hands, and then ran away at top speed!

"He's dropped the box!" exclaimed
Rachel, darting down to it.

Kirsty and Selena were close behind
her. Selena transformed the box to its
Fairyland size with a touch of her wand.

Then she waved her wand towards the
girls again.

"It's nice to have my own voice back!"
laughed Kirsty, rubbing her throat.

"Yes, I'm glad not to sound like a goblin

any more," said Rachel.

But before they could say anything else, the dustsheet on the statue beside them moved, and a green goblin face peered out!

Scary Shadows

Selena and the girls pressed themselves back against the tunnel wall. The goblin hadn't spotted them.

"He's gone!" hissed the goblin. "Now's our chance!"

The dustsheet slipped to the ground, and the girls gasped. Instead of a statue, they saw six goblins standing on each others' shoulders. They were wobbling precariously.

"I've had enough of sleepovers!" wheezed the goblin at the bottom. "Let's get out of here!"

They jumped down and scampered out of the tunnel. The girls heaved sighs of relief.

"Thank goodness!" said Rachel. "Jack Frost and the goblins have gone, and we've found the Sleepover Snack Box. Everything is back to normal."

"You've both been wonderful!" said Selena, hugging them tightly. "I am so happy to have all my magical objects back where they belong!"

"And we're happy to have helped," said Kirsty, hugging her back.

"I must take the Sleepover Snack Box to Fairyland," said Selena. "But I'll never forget what you have done for me today – and for sleepovers all over the world!"

She waved her wand, and in a flash of fairy dust the girls had returned to their human size.

"Goodbye," said Selena with a beaming smile. "I hope I'll see you again one day!"

"We hope so too!" said the girls together. "Goodbye!"

The air filled with shimmering golden fairy dust, and when it cleared, Selena had gone. Rachel and Kirsty smiled at each other happily, and then the sound of applause filled the air.

"That must mean that the story is over!" gasped Kirsty. "Quick!"

They raced out of the tunnel and slipped back into their places – just as Mr Ferguson turned to look at them!

"Did you enjoy it, girls?" he asked.

"It was a very exciting adventure!" said Rachel with a grin.

Just then, Charlotte appeared with two delivery men. They were carrying huge catering trays filled with delicious-smelling food.

"The delivery van was caught in a traffic jam," Charlotte explained to Mr Ferguson. "But the food's here now!"

She whisked the curtain aside and revealed a long banqueting table. The delivery men laid out dishes filled with cheese sandwiches, samosas and sausage rolls.

There were bowls of crisps and salad, pots
of jelly, tiny jugs of cream, platters of iced
cupcakes and masses of strawberries and
blueberries.

"Time for the feast!" Charlotte
announced.

All the children rushed to the table in excitement. Rachel and Kirsty chatted quietly about their adventures as they snacked on the wonderful food. In an amazingly short time, every single morsel had been eaten.

"Now it really is time for bed..." said
Charlotte.

There were groans from everyone, and
her eyes twinkled.

"... after a game of hide-and-seek, of
course!" she said with a laugh.

There was a loud cheer, and the
children picked up their lanterns and
got into pairs again.

"This has been one of the most exciting adventures yet," said Kirsty as they set off back up to the museum. "So much has happened today!"

"I'm really glad that we found all the magical objects in time," Rachel added. "Now we can relax and enjoy the sleepover."

"And the game of hide-and-seek," said Kirsty with a happy smile. "It's the perfect end to a truly magical adventure!"

**Now it's time for Kirsty and Rachel
to help...**

Honor the Happy Days Fairy

Read on for a sneak peek...

"We're here, Kirsty!" Rachel bounced up
and down in her seat with excitement
as she pointed out of the coach window.
"Look, that sign says *Golden Palace*."

Kirsty beamed at her friend. "I can't
believe we get to spend a whole week in
a *real* palace," she sighed happily. "I'm
beginning to feel like a princess already!"

There were cheers and whoops as
the other children on the coach also
spotted the sign. Golden Palace, a large
and beautiful stately home, was in the
countryside just outside the village of
Wetherbury where Kirsty lived. The house

was open to the public, but Kirsty had never visited it before. However, during the spring holidays the house was holding a special Kids' Week, and Kirsty had invited Rachel to come to Golden Palace with her.

"I can't wait to see our bedroom," Rachel said eagerly as the coach drove through the tall wrought-iron gates. "Imagine staying in a room that was once used by princes and princesses!"

"And I wonder what activities we're going to be doing this week," Kirsty added. "I hope we get to do lots of princess-type things!"

The coach trundled over a drawbridge and then began to wind its way slowly through the enormous grounds. Like all the other children on the coach, Rachel and Kirsty stared excitedly out of the window, straining to catch their first glimpse of Golden Palace. But there were lots of amazing things on the way to the house that caught their attention, too.

"Look, a petting zoo!" Kirsty exclaimed as they drove past a field of tiny Shetland ponies and little white goats...

Read Honor the Happy Days Fairy to find out what adventures are in store for Kirsty and Rachel!

Meet the
Friendship Fairies

When Jack Frost steals the Friendship Fairies' magical objects, BFFs everywhere are in trouble! Can Rachel and Kirsty help save the magic of friendship?

www.rainbowmagicbooks.co.uk

Calling all parents, carers and teachers!
The Rainbow Magic fairies are here to help
your child enter the magical world of reading.
Whatever reading stage they are at, there's
a Rainbow Magic book for everyone!
Here is Lydia the Reading Fairy's guide to
supporting your child's journey at all levels.

Starting Out

Our Rainbow Magic Beginner Readers are perfect for first-time readers who are just beginning to develop reading skills and confidence. Approved by teachers, they contain a full range of educational levelling, as well as lively full-colour illustrations.

Developing Readers

Rainbow Magic Early Readers contain longer stories and wider vocabulary for building stamina and growing confidence. These are adaptations of our most popular Rainbow Magic stories, specially developed for younger readers in conjunction with an Early Years reading consultant, with full-colour illustrations.

Going Solo

The Rainbow Magic chapter books – a mixture of series and one-off specials – contain accessible writing to encourage your child to venture into reading independently. These highly collectible and much-loved magical stories inspire a love of reading to last a lifetime.

www.rainbowmagicbooks.co.uk

"Rainbow Magic got my daughter reading chapter books. Great sparkly covers, cute fairies and traditional stories full of magic that she found impossible to put down" - Mother of Edie (6 years)

"Florence LOVES the Rainbow Magic books. She really enjoys reading now" - Mother of Florence (6 years)

The Rainbow Magic Reading Challenge

Well done, fairy friend – you have completed the book!
This book was worth 10 points.

See how far you have climbed on the
Reading Rainbow opposite.

The more books you read, the more points you will get,
and the closer you will be to becoming a Fairy Princess!

How to get your Reading Rainbow
1. Cut out the coin below
2. Go to the Rainbow Magic website
3. Download and print out your poster
4. Add your coin and climb up the Reading Rainbow!

There's all this and lots more at
www.rainbowmagicbooks.co.uk

You'll find activities, competitions, stories, a special
newsletter and complete profiles of all the
Rainbow Magic fairies. Find a fairy with your name!